# WELCOME TO
# YOUR **AMAZING** adventures™

Inside awaits an adventure that only you can have. It takes place in faraway, long ago lands. Monsters, sorcerers, and evil kings may oppose you, but you have the power to outwit them all. Your skill at pathfinding can steer you through all the perils, natural and otherwise, that stand in your path. If you are a good explorer of the mazes that block your journey, you'll win through in the end.

And if you get caught in the pitfalls of a maze, you can retrace your steps and try to find a better way out. That way, your skill determines the outcome.

You can be the hero, and save the island from the evil forces that threaten it.

If you're ready to go for it, turn the page and see what challenges await you.

Good luck!

# ISLAND OF FEAR

by
Richard Brightfield

Illustrated by Paul Abrams

## TOR

### A TOM DOHERTY ASSOCIATES BOOK

Copyright © 1984 by Richard Brightfield
Cover art and interior illustrations copyright © 1984 by Paul
and Karen Abrams
Mazes copyright © 1984 by Richard and Glory Brightfield

YOUR AMAZING ADVENTURES™ is a trademark
of Richard Brightfield

A Tor Book, published by arrangement with
Bluejay Books Inc.
Published by Tom Doherty Associates, 8-10 W. 36th Street,
New York, New York 10018

A Bluejay Books Production

First printing, December 1984

ISBN: 0-812-56038-8
CANADIAN ISBN: 0-812-56039-6

Printed in the United States of America

## ATTENTION!

You are about to enter an exciting world of sword and sorcery. *You* are the hero or heroine. You will have many adventures and face many dangers, but be especially careful going through the mazes—a wrong turn may be your last.

Once you have started on a path inside a maze, DON'T GO BACK—unless you reach a dead end. Finally, you will either get through the maze or enter a trap. Turn to the page indicated to discover your fate.

*You* are an adventurer. You are on your ship sailing into the Western Sea toward the chain of spice islands far to the west.

It is early morning, and the first rays of the sun are painting long, thin bands of scarlet low on the horizon to the east. Now out of sight beneath the edge of the sea, is the city of Trangor where you recently saved its king from the evil sorcerer, Kralux. Thea, your friend and partner, comes up on the rolling deck.

"Teppin is fixing some hot breakfast for us," she says. "He figures we need something to raise our spirits this second morning out of sight of land."

There is a crash below and some curses from Teppin, the only other person aboard.

"Sounds like he's got his hands full down there," you say. "I hope he doesn't set us on fire with the charcoal stove."

Soon a face appears at the hatch—and then two hands, each with a bowl of steaming porridge.

"Here! Grab these," says Teppin, "before they get swept overboard. I made them with honey and spice."

"Speaking of spices," Thea says, quickly grabbing her bowl, "we're supposed to be adventurers, not spice traders."

"Aye," says Teppin, "but the spice

trading gives us the appearance of re-
spectability. Anyway, searching the islands
for spices may prove to be adventure enough
for all of us."

"You think we're going to run into
trouble?" Thea asks.

"That could very well be," Teppin says,
"and furthermore, I don't like the looks of
that bank of clouds to the west. There's
something brewing over there. I can feel it in
the air."

"You think it's a storm?" you ask.

"Aye! And not an ordinary one either,"
Teppin answers. "You see that scud—those
small, vapor-like clouds—racing just over the
surface of the water up ahead, they're a dire
warning for the seaman."

"And the waves are certainly getting
choppy," Thea says.

"Do you think we should turn back
towards Trangor?" you ask Teppin.

"It would do us no good," he answers.
"That storm is coming our way too fast."

"What can we do?" Thea asks.

"Don't worry," Teppin says. "I've ridden
out many a storm in my day. When it comes,
we'll rig a small storm sail and take turns at
the tiller."

As Teppin is talking, the bank of clouds
rises higher. Soon they are looming overhead.

The wind has risen to a shriek so that you have to shout to be heard.

"Best we first furl the mainsail!" Teppin shouts, "before we loose it overboard."

You and Thea quickly undo the rope lines and the large square sail slides down the mast. Just as quickly, you wrap the sail around the horizontal boom and while holding on to keep from being blown overboard yourselves, you tie everything tight.

As you are finishing, a huge wave appears off of your starboard bow and towers over you like a small mountain of water. Teppin jumps to the tiller and swings the ship around to meet it, bow first. For a moment the wave seems like it's going to crash down on you, but then your boat is lifted up into the air by the wave. As you reach the crest you can see the boiling surface of the gray-green sea stretching in all directions. The jagged patterns of waves look like miniature mountain ranges, and the wind is blowing long spumes of foam from their peaks. Then you are hurtling down the other side of the wave into another trough. After that, the waves are high but not as high as that one.

"Whew! That was close!" Thea shouts above the wind.

"That was a freak wave!" Teppin shouts.

"They are unusual, but we'd better keep a close watch in case there's another. If one ever caught us broadside, we'd be done for."

Teppin motions for you to take the tiller while he goes forward to rig a storm sail, and Thea goes below to check the inside of the hull.

Go to next page.

*Find your way through the storm maze. And remember what it says on page 5.*

Go to page
106

Go to page
108

Go to
page
14

Start

You made it through the storm, but your ship is a wreck. The mast is split off near its base and jagged splinters of wood are all that's left of it. The rest of the mast, as well as sail and rigging, have been swept overboard. Most of the tiller is missing, and sections of the railing have broken off and are gone. The space below decks is filled with water. Only the fact that the boat is built of wood and that you have been bailing continuously—to the point of exhaustion—has kept the boat from sinking. Teppin, for the umpteenth time, hands up a canvas pail of water. You take it and pour it over the side. Then you slump wearily down on the deck.

You look out over the ocean. It's now relatively calm—the surface is a bit choppy with gusts of wind now and then, but nothing like it was during the storm. Thea is sitting, propped up against what's left of the hatchway.

"What do we do now?" she sighs.

"I don't know," Teppin says, pulling himself up through the hatch and out of the chest-high water below, "but at least we're still afloat."

"Barely," Thea says.

"Just a bit of a problem," Teppin says laughing, "but not hopeless. I'll admit that we have no sail and no tiller, and what's left of our supplies are awash below. The casks of fresh water are split and contaminated with sea water—"

"I get the picture!" you interrupt. "The thing now is to decide what to do. We have to try and reach land—but without a sail...."

Teppin is leaning over the edge of the boat with his hand dangling down into the water. "We're in a fast moving current that's taking us somewhere," he says. "Even if we still had our sail, I don't think it would help us much. We'll just have to wait and see where this current is going."

Go to next page.

The storm is now in a bank of clouds far to the east, tinted pink by the sunset. And to the west, golden-edged banners of crimson are unfurled against the sun sinking into the sea.

"We'll get a good rest tonight," Teppin says, "and figure things out in the morning."

That night, you all sleep on deck under a vast carpet of stars. You awake with a start during the night, but there is only the sound of Thea breathing peacefully, an occasional snore from Teppin, and the gentle rhythm of the water lapping against the sides of the boat. You sink back into a peaceful sleep.

Bright sunlight wakes you up the next morning. Teppin is standing at the bow, gazing intently to the south, his hand shielding his good eye.

"There's land there, all right," he says. "Luckily we're drifting in that direction."

"I don't see anything," you say, "except a small patch of clouds on the horizon."

"That's it," Teppin says. "That kind of cloud only forms over an island."

"I wonder where we are?" Thea, now awake, asks.

"It's hard to say," Teppin says. "We were swept way off course by that storm. The way this current is carrying us, we should reach that island soon enough. In the meantime, I think we should bail out the ship and get it back in order."

All of you work for hours, with Teppin handing up bucketfuls of water to you, and then you handing them to Thea, who dumps them overboard. When most of the water has been emptied out below, you start bringing up all your stores to the deck to dry out. Miraculously, your small, collapsible coracle— a small boat made of skins—is still in good shape, complete with two short oars still tied to it with a length of rope.

Go to next page.

The sun is rising higher and higher, and now you can just make out the coastline of an island. By noon, with the sun almost directly overhead, you can clearly see the shore and the low, flat mountains behind. But in front of the shore, separating you from it, are row upon row of huge, tall rocks. You can see the waves breaking against them, and throwing up columns of white spray against the stone.

"I've never seen anything like it," Thea says. "Can we get through them without being smashed to bits. We don't have a sail or anything to navigate with. Even the tiller is busted."

"I have an idea," says Teppin. "Let's tie the coracle to the bow and tow the ship to shore. I'm afraid that I'm too heavy for the coracle, so it's up to you."

"Those rocks are coming up fast!" Thea exclaims.

"Right!" Teppin says, pushing the now assembled boat of skins overboard and helping you climb in. You quickly tie the length of rope to the bow and start to row for all you're worth. But getting through the rocks isn't that easy. Some of them are too close together to go between. You have to pick your route carefully to keep from getting stuck or being dashed against the rocks by the waves.

Go to next page.

*Find your way through the maze of rocks. But be careful! One misjudgment may be your last.*

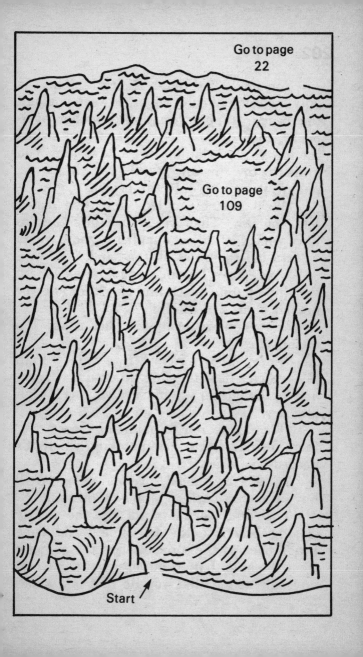

Go to page
22

Go to page
109

Start

You made it through the rocks! There is only a stretch of calm water between you and the beach. Teppin tosses the anchor overboard, then dives into the water and swims the few yards to land. Thea follows him. You untie the tow line and row the coracle ashore, pulling it well up onto the beach.

"We'll stretch our legs and then rest a bit," you say. "Then we can use the coracle to ferry what's left of our supplies to shore where we can lay them out on the sand."

"Aye," says Teppin, "and later we'll haul the ship up onto beach and check for loose or broken planks in the hull."

"How can we do that?" Thea asks. "It's awfully heavy."

"Easy," Teppin says. "If we wait for high tide we can float the ship up onto the beach and let the tide go out under it, leaving it high and dry."

"We can search through the woods over there for oak to cut new planking where it's needed," you say.

"And a new mast," Teppin says. "We'll have the ship back in shape in no time."

You and Teppin walk up the gently sloping beach to the tree line while Thea heads back in the coracle to get the supplies from the ship. Unfortunately, you don't find any oak trees. What you do find is a small jungle of interwoven thorn bushes that make an impenetrable barrier between the beach and the woods. You walk along it for quite a ways, looking for an opening. You are just about to turn back, when Teppin finds one.

"Look at this, over here!" he shouts. "Somebody or something has cut a narrow pathway through the thorn bushes."

"You're right," you say, coming up next to Teppin. "It looks like it goes in a ways and then divides into two paths—one going right and one going left."

"Do you think we should follow it and see where it goes?" Teppin asks.

"We'd better leave it alone," you say. "We have better things to do than get stuck in that tangle of thorns."

"I agree," says Teppin. "Best we get back and help Thea with the supplies on the beach."

When you get back, you find that Thea has already made two trips and has most of the things from the ship out on the ground.

"I didn't know we had that much stuff," Teppin says, laughing.

"I found my whip coiled up neatly and safely in the hold, and look, I found your slingshot too," Thea tells you.

"Now that we're back on land, we may have need of them," you say.

"And what are those I see!" Teppin exclaims. "Those are fish... where—"

"They were somehow washed into the boat during the storm," Thea says. "I found them when I started cleaning out the jumble of things in the hold."

"Aha!" exclaims Teppin, "and they'll make quite a good dinner."

"Something I sure can use," you say. "I'll start collecting driftwood for a fire."

As the red ball of the sun sinks into the ocean, Teppin manages to start up the fire with sparks from his flints, which he always carries in a special pocket. Then, using his long knife, he quickly scales and cleans the fish for roasting over the fire on sticks.

It's dark when you finish eating. The fire throws long shadows across the beach, all the way up to the dense bushes that fence it off. For a second you could swear that you

see two small eyes glint in the bushes. But that's impossible. Even a small animal would find it hard to squeeze through those brambles.

Thea yawns and stretches out on the sand.

"I don't know about you two," she says, "but *I* could sleep for days."

All of you make yourselves as comfortable as you can on the beach. The fire has died down to glowing embers and overhead the heavens blaze with stars, the bright trail of the milky way arching across the sky. Soon you are all asleep.

You half wake up at the first pale light of dawn. Immediately, you sense that something is wrong. You look over at Teppin, still sleeping peacefully close to the charred remains of the campfire. Then you look over to see how Thea is doing. But you don't see her. You prop yourself up on your elbow for a better look. Thea is gone! At first though you are not too alarmed. After all, she could have gotten up and walked down the beach to stretch her legs. But when you go over to where she had been sleeping, you see that the sand all around that spot has been trampled by... what! You can just make them out in the dim light—but that's what they are—tiny footprints! You rush over and shake Teppin awake.

"Thea is gone!" you exclaim. "I think she's been kidnapped by children."

Teppin is fully awake at once. He jumps up and runs over the where Thea had been sleeping. The light is a little better now as he kneels down to examine the footprints.

"No," he says, "I don't think that these are the footprints of children. They look like the footprints of pygmies."

"Pygmies?" you say.

"Yes," Teppin says, "I've run into them many times, going back to my buccaneering days. They inhabit many of the islands of these seas. They have an uncanny knack for predicting the weather. Many pirate captains kept one aboard for that purpose."

"But how did they snatch Thea without waking her—or us?" you ask.

"They can move as quietly as shadows," Teppin says. "And walking on the soft sand they made no sound. They probably gagged her before she could wake up enough to cry out."

"But why—" you start.

"I don't know of any good reason why they would take her," Teppin interrupts, "or why they would grab her and not us. But they won't get away with it."

"The pygmy tracks lead down the beach

toward that opening in the bramble we found yesterday," you say. "They must have carried her—I don't see any of Thea's footprints in the sand."

Teppin puts his hand around the hilt of the long knife in his belt. "This is all I need," he says. "We can start at once."

"And all I need is this," you say, picking up your slingshot from where Thea had carefully laid it out the day before. You also take along Thea's whip. Somehow you know that she'll need it when you catch up with her.

Then as the morning sun pokes the edge of its golden disk above the horizon, you and Teppin run up the beach to the narrow entrance to the brambles. You slip into the opening. Soon you find that the going isn't going to be easy. There is a maze of passageways through the closely knit thorn bushes and the thorns catch at your clothes as you try to find your way through.

*Find your way through the maze of bushes. But be careful, their thorns may be deadly.*

Go to page
30

Go to
page
110

Start

You got through the thicket. You and Teppin are both scratched and bleeding, and your clothes are torn and in shreds. But at least you got through alive. Ahead of you, across a shallow stream is a village of small, round huts. A handful of pygmies are walking about. Each of them carries a strange-looking device in their belt. You and Teppin crouch down behind some large rocks at the edge of the stream and try to figure out what to do.

"They don't look too dangerous," you say. "They may have Thea tied up in one of those huts, let's—"

"Hold on," says Teppin. "They may not *look* dangerous, but believe me, those rangs in their belts can be deadly."

"Rangs?" you ask.

"They're throwing sticks," Teppin replies. "I've seen them in use—at a distance they can cut a man's head off clean as a whistle, if they catch him right. The inside edge of the rangs are set with sword-sharp chips of obsidian. The rangs, though, are not too good for fighting at close range."

"Then let's get over there in close and find out what happened to Thea," you say.

You and Teppin wade across the stream to the village. The cold, clear water soothes the stinging of the scratches and cuts on your legs. As you enter the village, you find that the conical roofs of the small houses rise no higher than your chins. Strangely enough, the pygmies hardly seem to notice you. Teppin stops one of them and tries a few words in one of the island languages that he knows. The pygmy just babbles unintelligibly for a moment and then runs away.

"Looks like we'll have to look in each of these huts," you say.

You head toward the low, arched doorway of one of the huts. You are about to look inside, when you hear a "psst" from another doorway off to your right. A small, scared-looking face is peering around the edge of the door—then a hand appears, beckoning for you to come in. You and Teppin walk over to the doorway and peer down.

"Come in! Quickly!" a high, bird-like voice chirps. "This is as dangerous for me as it is for you."

"At least someone around here speaks our language," Teppin says, as he gets down on his hands and knees to crawl in. He takes out his long knife and holds it defensively as he does. You follow.

The inside of the hut is windowless and dark. A smooth, dirt floor is covered with straw mats and a low couch runs almost all the way around the inside against the wall. As your eyes get used to the dim light, you see the pygmy, now seated cross-legged by the door.

"My name is Tsing," he says. At least this is the way you hear it. "I am a friend," he adds.

"How is it that you speak our language?" Teppin asks.

"Not long ago, I sailed on one of your big ships," Tsing says. "I made a long journey and then returned here. The captain asked me each day what the weather would be the next. I told him. He did not want me to leave, but ..."

"We want to know what happened to our friend," you say. "We know your people kidnapped her."

"They did," replies Tsing. "And I am ashamed of them. But they live in fear—both of the Dirnl and the sorceress, Ferota."

"Dirnl? Ferota? Who are they?" you ask.

"Ferota wields an evil power over this island," says Tsing, "and the Dirnl are her followers. The only ones on this island that she does not control are the pirates in the tall ships anchored on the other side of the island. These she lets do as they like since they bring her captives for sacrifice."

"What about our friend?" you ask.

"I'm afraid that my people sold her to the Dirnl. They in turn will give her to Ferota.

"Let's go after them!" you exclaim, crawling toward the door.

"Wait!" Tsing exclaims. "The villagers have been paid by the Dirnl to kill you when you try to leave. You will be at the mercy of their rangs."

"Then what should we do?" you ask Tsing. "We have to rescue our friend."

"I will help you," says Tsing. "There may be a way to escape from the village, though it is also a dangerous one. But with luck we will succeed."

"We?" you say.

"Yes," says Tsing. "I will come with you."

"All right then," says Teppin, "tell us what to do."

"Just outside the village start the burrows of the giant Sorm. They are like what you call ... worms."

"Worms!" you exclaim. "How can we fit into worm holes?"

"These are very large," says Tsing. "I and my people can walk upright in their burrows, though you two may have to crawl. If we are lucky, we can get far enough away in them to escape."

"What about the Sorm?" Teppin asks, "won't they try to stop us?"

"At this season," Tsing says, "They go back to the sea to mate. Soon they will return to start a new life cycle under the earth."

"Then what are the dangers you mentioned?" you ask.

"I am not sure," says Tsing, "I have only heard stories..."

"Don't worry about it," Teppin interrupts. "The worm holes look like our best chance of getting out of here."

"We must wait for dark," Tsing says, "and move before the moon rises. In the meantime, you be my guest and stay here. I will go and find you some food. I think I know something you will like."

Go to next page.

Tsing scoots out of the door. Not long afterwards he returns with two steaming bowls of . . . something! You taste it cautiously. Whatever it is, it's delicious.

While you are eating, Tsing goes out again. When he comes back, he is carrying a basketful of leaves.

"Rub these on your cuts and scratches," he says, "they will make them feel better."

He's right. Not only do they feel better, but the cuts begin to heal as soon as the leaves touch them. After that, you rest, hoping all the time that Thea is still alive and that you can rescue her.

As soon as it is dark, you quietly follow Tsing around to the back of the hut and then into a field. Suddenly, there is a shout from the village. You hear a rang whiz through the air inches from your head. Then just as suddenly, Tsing pulls you down into a hole in the ground. You and Teppin find yourselves crawling through the dank tunnels of the Sorm. Tsing is still with you, but the other pygmies don't try to follow.

When you are a safe distance inside, Tsing pulls the cover off of a small, finely woven basket. Inside of the basket are a number of glowing insects. They give off a faint, greenish light. As your eyes get used to it you can make out the outlines of the tunnel.

You see that it branches a short distance ahead.

"Which way do we go?" you ask Tsing.

"I don't know," Tsing says, "I have never tried to follow these any further than this."

It's up to you to find the way through the maze of Sorm tunnels to safety.

Go to next page.

*Find your way through the tunnels, but watch out for the dangers that Tsing hinted at.*

Go to page 112

Go to page 40

Go to page 111

Start

Finally, you are out of the Sorm maze. You find yourselves at the bottom of a high, sloping hill. It curves away from you in both directions as if it were the outside of a giant cone. Furthermore, as you look up, you see a faint shaft of light shining up into the sky from the top. There seems to be a kind of throbbing in the air. You can't actually hear it, but you feel it.

"That's a strange light up there," Teppin says. "But it can't be from the moon. There's the moon just rising over that low hill behind us.

"Let's climb up and see what it is and—" you start. Then you notice that Tsing is shaking with fear, his eyes as wide open as saucers.

"What is it?" you ask him.

Tsing doesn't seem to be able to answer. He just crouches close to the ground with his hands covering his head.

"Snap out of it, Tsing!" Teppin orders. "Whatever it is, we can handle it."

This doesn't do much good. In fact, it just makes Tsing start whimpering.

"All right then," Teppin says. "We'll just leave ·you here and go up and see for yourselves."

This does have an effect. Tsing shakes his head violently, at the same time he grabs hold of Teppin's arm.

"OK, here we go," Teppin says, starting up the slope and pulling Tsing after him.

By the time you all get to the top of the hill, Tsing has pulled himself together.

You look down on an incredible scene. Below is a broad natural amphitheater, probably once the crater of a fiery mountain. In the center is a perfectly round lake. And in the center of the lake is a temple, brightly lit by burning torches. Around the lake stand concentric circles of black robed and hooded figures, all swaying back and forth and chanting in deep tones. That was the throbbing that you felt below the hill. The chanting is now quite loud and almost hypnotic. You all duck down and flatten yourselves behind a ridge along the top of the crater.

"This must be the valley of the magic jewel," Tsing whispers, "I've never seen the valley before, but I know what it is from the many stories I've heard about it."

"The magic jewel? What is that?" you whisper to Tsing.

"I'm not sure," he says, "I've never seen it, but—" An edge of fear is coming back into his voice.

Tsing suddenly stops talking and gazes speechless up into the sky. Starting to form over the temple like a luminous cloud is the giant image of a human head. It's face is that of a woman with deadly-looking fangs protruding from her mouth. It gradually solidifies and hangs there in the air.

"It's Ferota," Tsing whimpers while trying to dig himself into the ground.

For a moment you can feel the fear in yourself as her eyes burning with white-hot fire like two burning gates of hell, turn in your direction. You are not sure if these "eyes" can see or not, but you and Teppin both inch backward from the ridge and flatten out as much as possible. Your last look into the crater gives you a view of the monks bowing to the terrible apparition above them. Then a booming voice comes from the huge image of Ferota.

"Listen, my slaves, I have happened upon a soul of great strength and power. It is in the body of a young girl—now my captive. She will be sacrificed to the jewel at the rise of the full moon two nights hence. The jewel will remain here until all is ready at the monastery of death. My servant Groar will bring it to us just before the sacrifice. Thenceforth it will remain with renewed power at the monastery."

This announcement ends with a piercing cry that cuts through you like a knife of ice.

You can feel your legs shaking as it rises to a higher and higher pitch. Suddenly, there is an incredible burst of light—so bright that it might have blinded you if you had been looking at it. Fortunately, you, Teppin, and Tsing, all have your faces half buried in the ground.

Then all is quiet! The giant face of Ferota vanishes. Cautiously you pull yourself back up to the rim and look back down at the temple. The hooded figures have started to form in a long line and are marching to the other side of the crater. There you see a dip in its edge and a long ramp leading up to it. Then, the luminous figure of Ferota, her normal size this time, floats out of the temple and across the lake. It enters a closed palanquin suspended on poles supported by several of the hooded figures. Behind it you notice a large basket carried by another group of monks. All of this is so far away that you have trouble making out the details, but you have a hunch.

"I'll bet that Thea is in that basket they're carrying," you whisper to Teppin. "If we could only get to her."

"I'd say we're slightly outnumbered at the moment," Teppin says, "but our time will come, never fear."

You watch as the last of the figures leave

the crater.

"Let's follow them," you say. "There must be something that we can do."

"I think we'd better get a closer look at that temple before we do anything else," says Teppin. "We may learn something that will help us."

"I guess you're right," you say, "but I sure hate to see them going off with Thea like that."

As you start to work your way down the inside slope of the crater, you notice that the eastern sky is beginning to pale.

When you reach the edge of the lake, you see that Tsing is standing behind you shaking again and staring over at the temple with a look of horror on his face.

"I don't understand it," Teppin says, turning back to Tsing. "You weren't afraid in the village when you took us under your wing, or even in the tunnels of the Sorm. But since we've been near this valley, you've been scared to death.

"I know," Tsing says, his teeth still chattering, "I can't really understand it myself. My people call it 'the fear.' It comes over us when we go too far from our village. It has something to do with Ferota and her sorcery. It's as if she has put a spell on us."

"I suspected as much," you say. "I've

had experience with many such spells."

"Well, spells or not," says Teppin, "let's swim over and see what we can find out in that temple."

"No, I can't!" Tsing exclaims.

"Then stay here and wait for us," you say, getting ready to dive into the lake.

"I will," he says. "Be careful!"

You and Teppin dive into the refreshingly cool and clear water of the lake and swim toward the island. Minutes later, you pull yourselves up onto a marble platform that extends into the lake from the front of the temple. You pull yourselves, dripping, out of the water. You check your belt to make sure that your slingshot is still hanging on one side and Thea's whip on the other. You and Teppin stand there for a moment. All is quiet except for the sound of water dripping down onto the platform from your torn clothes, and the chirps of a few birds way up somewhere inside the broad dome that caps the circle of thirteen tall pillars in front of you. Under this canopy is another structure, a perfect cube of polished stone. You and Teppin walk over to examine it.

"I don't see any doors or openings," you say, "not even a crack."

"I don't either," Teppin says, "but I'll bet that Ferota came out of this thing."

Off to one side, resting on the temple platform, is a large perfectly round ball of polished stone.

"I have an idea," Teppin says. "I'm going to see what kind of stuff this cube is made of."

Teppin picks up the round stone. It's so heavy that Teppin, even with his considerable strength, has difficulty hefting it. With a grunt of effort, he hurls it at the cube. As the ball bounces off, there is a sound like a large gong being struck. It vibrates for several seconds. The ball itself rolls along the smooth platform, almost back to Teppin's feet. All is silent again. Then suddenly, there is a muted roar from inside the cube and a crack—the outline of a large door—starts to form on the side. The door swings open, and a huge figure, half-man and half-beast comes out. With another roar, it comes charging at you. But you are ready. From the moment that the crack started to appear, you had slipped the slingshot from your belt and seated a stone. You let fly as the beast comes at you, hitting it right between the eyes. This stops the beast for a moment. It shakes its head and lets out a blood-curdling cry. Almost immediately, you hit it with another stone, near the first hit. The beast grunts and shakes its head again, not hurt but puzzled by what is happening.

And then, wham! Teppin has come up

behind the beast and scores a direct hit on the back of its head with the large stone ball. The fierce eyes of the monster glaze over and it falls with a crash to the stone platform. Teppin runs over and puts his ear close to the beast's face.

"Whatever it is," he says, "it's still breathing. I think it'll be out for awhile. Now, let's see what's inside that cube."

Inside is a small room in the center of which is a stairway leading down under the temple. Without hesitation, you and Teppin descend the stairway to a corridor below. The walls are luminous and you can see that it goes for a way and then divides into several different passageways. You realize that it's probably some kind of maze.

Go to next page.

*Find your way through the temple maze. Be careful, there may be things lurking down there that you're not prepared for.*

You come out of the maze into a large chamber. The walls, like those of the corridors you just left, are luminous. At the far side of the chamber is a large multi-armed idol. Its arms are joined like the legs of some huge insect and end in "hands" with long, thin claws. The ugly idol sits cross-legged on a platform of black stone. In addition, it glows from within in shades of blood red and orange as if carved from crystal and lit by a red hot flame. Yet there is no heat coming from it. It's ice cold in the chamber.

Then you notice that two of the idol's hands are cupped in its "lap" and are holding a beautiful, multi-faceted jewel the size of an egg. Teppin sees it too. He goes over and tries to pick it up, but as he touches it, it flares with a blinding light and Teppin is struck by some kind of invisible force. He jerks his hand away from the jewel and stands there in pain for a moment, gasping for breath.

"That thing packs a wallop!" he exclaims.

"Are you all right?" you ask.

"I'm all right now," Teppin answers. "Somehow I think we can use that jewel. We'll take it with us."

"Take it with us!" you repeat. "You barely touched it and—"

"I know," Teppin says, "but maybe if we got it out of the idol's hands. Lend me that

whip for a moment."

Teppin takes the whip and, with a crack, jars loose the jewel. It flies up into the air and crashes to the stone floor of the chamber. Do you imagine it, or do you hear a scream somewhere.

You kneel down over the jewel and give it a slight touch with your finger. You get a jolt of pain through your finger and at the same time a beam of light suddenly shoots out from the jewel and shines on the smooth wall opposite. A picture—a moving one—begins to form. This makes even Teppin gasp and take a step backwards.

"What witchcraft is this!" he exclaims.

"Look," you say, "it's a picture of Ferota and her caravan. There . . . she's looking this way and . . . screaming?"

You can't hear anything, but from the picture of her mouth opening and closing and her arms thrashing about, it's obvious that she's in a rage. Then she seems to be shouting orders to her followers. They are all turning and heading . . . back your way?

"I don't like the looks of that, whatever it is," Teppin says.

"I think you're right," you say, "we'd better get out of here fast. Oh, and what about the jewel?"

"I think we just need something to carry it

in," Teppin says looking around the chamber. "What's that over there in the corner?"

You find a pile of robes, like the ones the Dirnl wear, and a small pouch, just the right size for the jewel. Using the handle of Thea's whip, you carefully nudge the jewel into the pouch and pull the drawstring tight. Once inside the pouch it doesn't seem to affect you. You tie the whip back on your belt and next to it, the pouch with the jewel.

"Let's take a couple of these robes with us," you say, "they could be useful."

You and Teppin find your way back through the maze to the stairway. When you come out on the surface again, the monster is still lying there. He is groaning and appears to be coming to.

Go to next page.

"What'll we do with him?" you ask.

"I guess we'll just leave him here," Teppin says. "I don't think that tying him up would do any good. He seems strong enough to break any kind of bonds that we could find."

"Our best bet then is to get away from here as quickly as possible," you say.

The two of you dive back into the lake and swim for the shore, holding the rolled up robes over your heads and out of the water. You can hear the jewel hissing in its pouch as it gets wet.

Tsing comes running over as you pull yourselves ashore. You don't tell him about the jewel right away, but as you unroll the hooded capes and start to put them on, Tsing lets out a screech and faints dead away.

"Poor little fella," Teppin says. "This whole thing has been too much for him."

"Actually, he is probably the bravest of his tribe," you say. "He has to be, the way he helped us escape. You can imagine how Ferota's curse must terrorize him."

"You're right," Teppin says. "Tsing after all is only human. He's probably reached the end of his endurance."

"We can't just leave him here, though," you say.

"He doesn't weigh more than a small bundle of firewood," Teppin says, hoisting

Tsing over his shoulder. "Let's head for that exit out of this place."

At the top of the small pass, you can see far across a broad plain. At the other side of it is the edge of a forest that stretches many leagues to a range of low mountains in the far distance. And heading out of the forest, though they appear as small dots at this distance, is what looks like Ferota's caravan heading back your way—and moving fast.

Fortunately, Tsing is stirring on Teppin's shoulder. Teppin eases him back down to the ground. As Tsing regains consciousness his eyes open as wide as saucers, but he doesn't pass out again.

"Welcome back," Teppin says. "We've got to get somewhere fast before Ferota and her goons arrive. Any suggestions?"

Tsing shakes his head as if to clear it for thinking. Then he gets to his feet and looks around.

"I don't know this part of the island too well," he says, "but I think that there are some old tin mines—not worked since Ferota gained power—over in that direction."

Tsing points way over to the right.

"That sounds like a good possibility," Teppin says. "If we get underground, we might have a better chance of defending ourselves."

You all hurry in that direction, Tsing leading the way. For the moment, his fears seem to have vanished.

After a half-hour or so, you reach a series of small mounds, each with a round hole at the base.

"Here we are," Tsing says.

"I don't know—" you start.

"Don't worry," Tsing says, "the tunnels are much larger underground. From stories that I've heard, the mines have all sorts of interconnecting tunnels. Some of them should lead toward the forest. I have friends there."

"It's worth a try," you say, squeezing into the largest hole that you can find. You are followed by Tsing and Teppin.

Tsing is right. You drop down into a fairly roomy tunnel. You can see that nearby it branches. Another maze.

*Find your way through the maze of mine shafts and tunnels. Don't forget that there may be dangers lurking even in an old, abandoned mine.*

Start

Go to
page
116

Go to page
60

Go to page
119

You push your way through a hatchway covered with old timbers and dirt. It falls away in a cloud of dust. You look up at a clear blue sky. You are out of the maze and out of the mines at last. You, Teppin, and Tsing climb a nearby hill and look around. You are at the edge of the plain, almost to the forest. Suddenly, Tsing gives a cry and points in the direction of the temple, now out of sight far back across the plain.

"What is it?" you ask him. "I don't see anything."

Tsing doesn't answer, but just keeps pointing.

"I see it," Teppin says, "a tiny dot moving this way."

"It's ... it's Groar," Tsing stutters, "He's after us."

"Groar?" you say, "Who's that?"

"He's the guardian of the temple," Tsing says.

"Oh, him," Teppin says. "We had a small run-in with him while you were waiting for us. How do you know his name?"

"He is well known and feared," Tsing says. "He is also known as the 'terrible one.'"

"You can really recognize him from this distance?" you ask. "All I can see is a tiny moving figure."

"My people can see very long distances,"

Tsing says.

"We'll get to the forest over there long before he does," Teppin says, "and then we'll easily lose him."

"Maybe," Tsing says, "but Groar is to be feared most in the forest. He was once one of the forest people himself."

"You mean the people of the forest all look like Groar!" you exclaim.

"No, no!" Tsing says in his high-pitched voice. "The forest people look much like me. Groar was once like me too. He changed, but that is a long story."

"It sounds like a *very* long story," you say.

"And one that we don't have time to hear right now," Teppin says. "I think we should get over into the forest as fast as we can. From the way that dot is growing, it looks like Groar is heading this way fast."

You all start out across the field between you and the forest. Twenty minutes later, you are there and hurrying down a wide path between the tall trees. Every so often, Tsing gives a loud whistle. Then suddenly, it's answered by a whistle from high above.

"We are close to a village," Tsing says. "In fact, we are directly beneath it."

You look straight up, but all you can see is a thick pattern of branches and leaves.

"Above us?" you say. "I don't see anything."

"You will," says Tsing. "I hope you're not afraid of heights. The village is in the tree tops."

"But how are we going to get up there?" Teppin asks. "The first branch on those trees is fifty feet up."

Tsing gives another whistle—actually a series of whistles that seem to be a language in themselves. Three ropes, each with a basket at the end, come dropping out of the canopy of leaves above.

"Climb in," Tsing says, "and they'll haul us up."

"I don't know," says Teppin, "I'm pretty heavy and—"

"Never fear," Tsing says. "Each of these ropes can hold three times your weight."

"If you say so," says Teppin, climbing into one of the baskets.

You are a bit nervous yourself but, with Groar on your trail and possibly not far away, you don't have much choice. As soon as you are in, the basket starts to rise at a fast speed. You duck involuntarily as it crashes through the canopy of leaves that hides the "town" from the ground far below. You find yourself in another world. The tiny houses are built at the very tops of the tall trees. They are all

connected by narrow, woven-rope walkways. The basket you are riding in comes to a stop beside one of them. You climb out carefully into the somewhat wobbly walkway and start toward the nearest tree house. Teppin and Tsing are right behind you.

You all go inside. Sitting on a stool by the window is an old man. He's the first pygmy that you've seen with a long, gray beard.

"I am Tuan," the man says, motioning with his hand for you all to be seated. "I am the village elder. News travels fast in the forest. I know that you are pursued by both Ferota and Groar. I will help you as much as I can, but I'm powerless against them."

"Thank you," you say.

"There is something else," Tuan says. "I know that you carry the jewel."

"Wha—what jewel?" Tsing says, a look of fear back in his eyes.

"Look, Tsing, we didn't want to tell you ..." you say, "but ..."

Tsing cringes, his hands to his throat, and his eyes wide with horror.

"Be calm my boy," Tuan says, putting his hand on Tsing's head. This seems to help. "The jewel is the seed of evil," Tuan goes on, "if it is not destroyed, and soon, there is no hope for any of us."

Almost without realizing it, you put your

hand on the pouch that holds the jewel. Destroy it? you think. No! I can't do that. It's too beautiful and too valuable. A feeling of anger at anyone who would want to destroy the precious jewel crosses your mind for a moment, like a dark cloud passing over the sun. Then it passes and you wonder why you ever thought that.

"The jewel must somehow be destroyed," Tuan says again, though I do not know how that can be done. The jewel will not allow itself to be destroyed. In addition, it is made of a substance so hard as to be indestructible."

"How about burying it, or tossing it into the sea," you suggest.

"No use," Tuan says, "it will always find its way to someone who is willing to use it for evil."

"Suppose we take it *far* out to sea and toss it overboard," says Teppin.

"The jewel will find a way," Tuan says. "Maybe it will have itself swallowed by a fish, which in turn will be caught by an unsuspecting fisherman. Or someday it would be washed onto the shore."

"Hm, I see what you mean," Teppin says, sitting with his fist on his chin in a pose of deep thought.

"Suppose I just carry it with me until, someday, I can find a way to stop its power," you say.

"No," Tuan says. "It would gradually take over your soul, as it did Ferota's."

"Ferota?" you say.

"Ferota was once a simple shepherd girl of our tribe," Tsing says, now recovered from the shock of knowing that you have the jewel. "A pygmy girl like the rest of our people."

"She's certainly not a pygmy now!" Teppin exclaims.

"I know," Tsing says. "One day, while she was in the fields, a black stone fell from the sky and landed near her. The stone was red hot. As it cooled, it cracked open and the jewel rolled out. Ferota let it cool completely, then picked up the jewel and took it home. She told no one about it, but kept it hidden under her bed. In the months that followed, she started to grow and gradually took on the form in which you see her today. She moved from the village to that island in the crater lake. As she gained in power, many left the tribes of the island and became Dirnl—her followers. They too grew in size as she took over *their* souls.

"What about Groar?" you ask.

"Ah, yes. Groar." Tuan says with a sigh. "He is my real son, and one of Ferota's first followers. He has changed since he..." Tuan chokes a little and can't go on. You can see the

pain in his eyes.

"Well, look," Teppin says, "Is there anything we can do?"

With an effort, Tuan pulls himself back together. "Yes," he says, "find the secret of the jewel and free my son."

"The secret?" you ask.

"If you can find the secret of its power," says Tuan, "it may be possible to destroy it."

"Anybody here have any ideas?" Teppin asks.

"Ferota herself said something about the jewel needing to be 'renewed,'" you say. "The ceremony was to take place at the monastery. Thea has probably been taken there. If we can get into that place, we may learn the secret, and free Thea at the same time."

"We should get going then," Tsing says.

You and Teppin look at each other. You know what the other is thinking.

"I think... it best that you stay here with Tuan," you say to Tsing. "You have been very helpful and very brave, but..."

"I understand. As we get closer to the monastery," Tsing says with a shudder, "I'll be less and less able to control my fear. It is wise that I stay here."

"Thank you, Tsing," you say with deep feeling. "Teppin and I owe you a lot."

"Good luck on finding your friend—and

the secret of the jewel," Tsing says, a tear in his eye.

"Now," Teppin says, "just how do we get to this monastery?"

"There is a network of rope bridges that go across the top of the forest in that direction," says Tuan. "Sometimes they are hard to follow, but I know you will find your way"

Tuan gives you a small package. "This is food," he says. "Eat it on your journey. It will nourish you."

Then Tsing and Tuan wave goodby as you start out over the series of rope bridges that lead toward the other side of the forest and the monastery.

Go to next page.

*Find your way across the maze of bridges. Be careful not to fall off, and watch out for Groar who is still after you.*

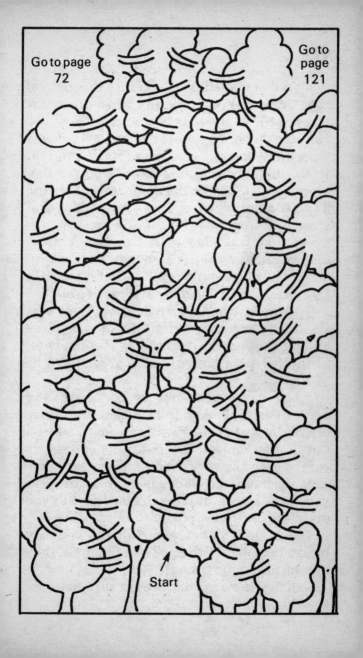

Go to page
72

Go to page
121

Start

You've made it safely across the maze of rope bridges. You are at the other side of the forest, still in the tops of the trees. Now you can see a broad desert-like valley covered with multi-colored, sculptured rocks. And far in the distance, clinging to the side of a flat-topped mountain, is the monastery. You and Teppin climb down a long rope ladder that stretches from the top of the trees to the ground at the edge of the forest. A short distance away the rocks begin.

"Whew!" Teppin exclaims, "I feel like I've been going for days without sleep."

"Almost two days, to be exact," you say.

"Let's see if we can find a cool place among those rocks over there," Teppin says. "I think I see a kind of cave carved into one of them."

The cave turns out to be larger and deeper than it looked from a distance. There is even a pool of clear water inside. You sink down into one of the natural depressions carved into the rock. Teppin does the same. You open up the package that Tuan gave you. Inside are a number of biscuits that you divide up with Teppin.

"Not much, but something," you say biting into one of them. Though small, they are surprisingly filling.

"They taste good," Teppin says between

munches.

You wash them down with some of the water from the pool.

"It's time we rested," Teppin says, "but first I have to do something. Oh, and by the way, lend me Thea's whip."

You sink quickly into sleep. An hour or so later, Teppin gently shakes you awake.

"I've prepared a little reception for Groar if he shows up," Teppin says, "I collected some of the heaviest loose rocks I could find and piled them over the entrance to the cave. The end of Thea's whip is tied around the one in the middle. The handle of the whip is over here where it hangs down. You see that white stone at the entrance. If Groar tries to come in, yank down on the whip just as he passes it. This will start all the rocks tumbling down. The white stone is a couple of feet past where the rocks will fall."

"But if the stone is not where the rocks will fall..." you say.

"Trust me," Teppin says, as he goes deeper into the cave to take his turn resting.

You crouch down near the mouth of the cave, listening for any sounds that would mean groar was trying to find you. You listen and listen. Soon you have a hard time keeping from dozing off. Then a slight crunching sound nearby jolts you wide

awake. You don't want to get Teppin. It might just be a small animal moving about. Then you hear a loud sniffing—that's getting closer. You get a climpse of a bald, green head bobbing among the nearby rocks. It's Groar!

Then he's at the entrance to the cave. He stops for a moment sniffing the air, trying to track your scent. He's standing right on the white rock. You yank on the whip. There is a loud, grinding sound as the rocks start to fall.

Groar's reflexes are quick. The moment he hears the rocks moving above him, he springs backwards—right into the path of falling rocks. Now you see why Teppin put the marker where he did.

Teppin comes running up seconds later. Groar is buried under the pile. He is growling and trying to dig his way out. Teppin grabs Thea's whip and pulls it free. Then both of you head out into the maze of rock formations that stands between you and the monastery. For Tuan's sake, you're glad that the rocks didn't kill Groar, but you hope that he is hurting enough to give you and Teppin a good head start.

*Find your way through the rock forma-
tion maze. But hurry, Groar may be after you
sooner than you think. And there may be
other dangers.*

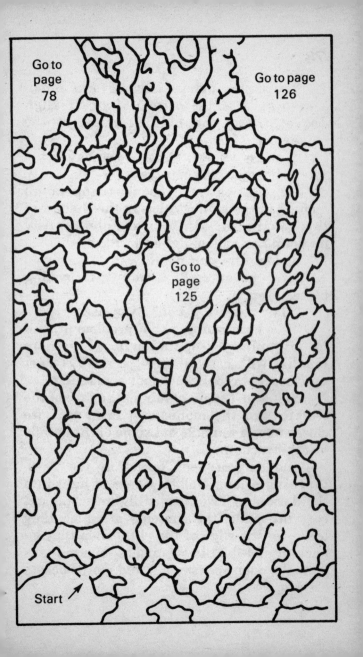

Go to
page
78

Go to page
126

Go to
page
125

Start

You are through the maze of rocks and in a deep gully at the bottom of a cliff. High above you is the hulking mass of the monastery.

"I guess we lost Groar," you say.

"I hope so," Teppin says.

Off to the east, the moon is rising—a full moon, but the monastery is in the shadow of the mountain. Only a couple of tiny pinpoints of yellow light show that there is life inside. Life *and* death.

"I've never seen a more evil looking place," Teppin says.

"How can we get in?" you ask.

"I've been running that problem around in my mind," Teppin says, "I'm more familiar with castles than you are. Let's get up closer. Maybe I can spot something."

You and Teppin climb up the face of the cliff toward the monastery. Soon you are close enough to make out some of the details of construction.

Suddenly a door opens in the base, throwing a long, yellow finger of light into the darkness. Two hooded figures come out carrying pails, the contents of which they toss over the edge of the cliff. Then they go back in and the light vanishes. Ten minutes later the door opens again and more buckets are emptied.

"That gives me an idea," Teppin says. "We're wearing robes just like the monks. We may be able to sneak in through the back door."

You and Teppin work your way up beside the door. You don't have to wait long. It opens and the monks come out. Two quick blows, one from you and one from Teppin, and they are out cold on the ground. You pick up one pail and Teppin the other. Then, pulling the hoods of your robes around your heads, you go through the door into the monastery. You enter a deserted basement room. Two corridors lead away from it. Both are dimly lit. Down one of them, you can hear talking. No sound comes from the other. You and Teppin put down your buckets and move quickly into the silent one. Soon it branches.

"We have to find where they are holding Thea," you say.

But soon you and Teppin realize that you've entered a maze of passages. There's nothing else for you to do except see where they lead.

*Find your way through the maze of basement passageways. Be especially careful. Remember that in the monastery of death anything can happen.*

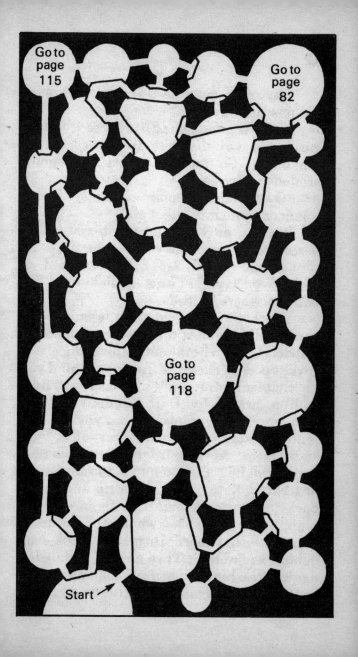

Go to page 115

Go to page 82

Go to page 118

Start

You and Teppin keep searching through the passageways.

"This is maddening," you say, "There must be a way to get to an upper level—or something. So far we've just been going around in circles.

"Over there!" Teppin exclaims, "there's a ladder built into the wall."

But just as you head for it, you hear a fierce growl down the corridor beyond.

"Sounds like Groar has tracked us down," you say. "Let's get up that ladder fast and see where it leads."

You both sprint over to the ladder and quickly climb up. At the top you push open a trapdoor and climb out into silence and darkness. You close the trapdoor behind you.

Suddenly, the space around you is filled with a bright light. It blinds you for a moment. Then you realize that you are on a kind of stage in the center of a vast auditorium. At the front of the stage is Ferota holding a scepter up in the air. Beams of light radiate out from its tip and reflect back down into the hall from a gilded ceiling high above you. The whole auditorium is packed with hooded Dirnl. You look back behind you and see Thea gagged and tied up against the high base of an idol like the one in the Temple of the Jewel. This one is bigger and if anything more hideous.

"So nice of you to come and bring the jewel for the sacrifice!" Ferota snarls. "I'll take it now."

"The jewel is mine! The power is mine!" you scream. At the same time, you seem far off hearing yourself saying this. A chill of fear goes through you—a fear beyond that of being menaced by Ferota and the Dirnl.

"Fool!" Ferota shouts. "You don't know what to do with the power. Give me the jewel at once or I'll cut this girl's throat from ear to ear." She runs over and holds a dagger at Thea's throat.

"Stop!" you cry. "I'll give you the jewel. Just take the dagger away."

Ferota reaches out her gloved hand for the jewel, a look of evil triumph on her face. At the same time, you deftly slip the jewel from its pouch into your slingshot. A fast shot and you hit Ferota between the eyes. The jewel seems to stick on her forehead for a few seconds. There is a loud crackling sound and miniature bolts of lightning play around her head. Her voice stops in mid-scream. She is suddenly paralyzed and stands there like a statue, still holding the scepter in the air.

Then the jewel drops to the floor. You quickly scoop it back into the pouch. While this has been going on, Teppin has freed

Thea from the idol. You yank open the trap
door. Groar's head suddenly pops up through
it like a jack-in-the-box. His mouth is open in
a roar, his fangs glistening in the light.
Almost without thinking, you empty the
pouch of its jewel into Groar's mouth. He lets
out a hideous shriek and drops like a stone to
the basement floor below. The hundreds of
Dirnl filling the auditorium don't seem to
understand what is going on or else Ferota's
paralysis has immobilized them too. In any
event, they just sit there as Teppin helps
Thea through the trapdoor and down the
ladder with you following. Groar is lying
unconscious at the bottom. The jewel has
fallen out of his mouth and is lying on the
floor near his head. You pause long enough
to get the jewel in its pouch. Then you all
rush back through the basement maze,
through the door, and out into the bright
moonlight, hurrying away from the monastery.

"It's so great to see you two," Thea says,
slightly out of breath, "I had almost given up
hope ... no, not really. I knew that somehow
you'd find me."

"We're not out of the soup yet," says
Teppin.

"But at least we're all together again,"
you say.

Several times as you hurry along, you

notice Thea looking at you with a funny expression on her face. "Can I ask you something?" she says.

"Sure," you say, "what is it?"

"I'm not really sure," she says, "but for some reason you look taller than Teppin. Do you think you've grown several inches since we left the boat, or has Teppin shrunk?"

"Thea's right!" Teppin exclaims, overhearing the question. "I'll bet it's that jewel you've been carrying. You'd better give it to me or Thea."

"No! *I'll* carry it!" you exclaim. "It's mine and I won't give it to anybody."

"What's going on here?" Thea asks.

"Nothing, nothing at all," Teppin says. "But I think we should stop and rest for awhile."

"Rest?" you say. "With Ferota and the Dirnl maybe after us."

"Look," Teppin says, "we've been going for days, with hardly any rest and..."

"All right," you say, "we'll stop for a bit. But the more distance we put between us and the monastery the better."

You all stop and sit under a tree. Up above, dark clouds have started rushing over the full moon. Somehow, the swirling forms of the clouds makes you dizzy. You feel faint. You're more tired than you thought, and soon you doze off into a deep sleep.

Some time later, you awake with a start. You immediately feel down at your belt. The jewel—it's gone. You spring to your feet and bellow out an anguished cry.

Teppin is standing a few feet away, hands on hips. Thea is behind him, a scared look on her face.

"Give it back to me!" you demand.

"If you want it, you'll have to fight me for it," Teppin says.

Angrily, you reach for your slingshot, but that's gone too.

"Teppin, you—" you start to say. Then suddenly you realize what you are saying, and what a hold the jewel was getting over you. You sink down to the ground, your face in your hands. Thea runs over to you.

"Are you all right," she asks.

"Yes...," you say, "I'm ... I'm sorry."

"Teppin and I were so worried," Thea says.

"From now on," Teppin says, "no one holds the jewel for more than a day at a time. I have a hunch that the evil force that's in the jewel, whatever it is, has to take over a soul or have a blood sacrifice every new moon to renew itself. If it doesn't it will—"

Suddenly, Teppin grabs at his side and grimaces in pain. He rips the diamond in its pouch from his belt and throws it on the ground. A thick, luminous fog rolls over all of you and the ground starts to shake under your feet.

"Fools!" you hear a deep, booming voice say from somewhere, "do you think I came all the way from another world just to have three petty creatures destroy me!"

A channel grows in the fog in front of you. As you watch, it divides into a maze of similar channels.

"First," the booming voice says, "we'll see how you do in the maze of death."

A burst of flame erupts behind you and spreads in your direction. You all have to run forward into the maze to keep from being engulfed.

"Haaa!" the voice gives out a terrible laugh. "If you stop or reach a dead end, you'll be burned to a crisp!" it screams.

You all rush deeper into the maze, the flames exploding and spreading behind you.

*Can you make it through the maze of death? It's your only chance to escape from the demon in the jewel.*

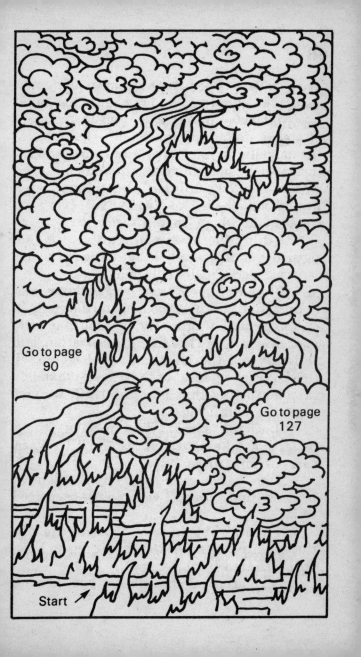

Go to page
90

Go to page
127

Start

You've escaped from the maze of death. You look behind you and the lethal fog bank has contracted into a wide, swirling column of smoke rising up into the air. It shines in the moonlight like some giant specter—an insect shape of monstrous size. Then, as you watch, it grows thinner and thinner, and finally vanishes. The jewel is still lying on the ground where Teppin threw it.

"I think the jewel realized that we had figured out its secret, that it needed to be renewed periodically," Teppin says.

"I have a hunch," you say, walking over to the jewel, still in its pouch, and dumping it on the ground. Cautiously, you touch it with your finger. There is a tingling sensation, but certainly not the jolt that it had before. "I think it used up most of the energy it had left in constructing that maze of death we just went through," you say.

"Just the same," Teppin says, "we'd better not take any chances. We'll let Thea carry it for awhile."

"Ugh!" Thea exclaims, "do I really have to carry that thing? I was almost sacrificed to it."

"I know," Teppin says, "but you are also the one least likely of the three of us to have been affected by it."

Suddenly, not far away, you hear a

crashing through the woods and an un-
mistakable growl—Groar's!

"Groar it seems still has some energy
left," you say. "Let's get going."

Teppin picks up the jewel with his hand
and puts it back in its pouch which he hands
to Thea. Then you all start running down the
path away from Groar. There is another
growl, closer this time, followed by a hideous
shriek from the same direction.

"Sounds like Ferota herself is in on the
chase this time," Teppin says.

You look back just as you cross a wide
clearing. Ferota and Groar are just coming
out of the woods on the other side. They look
smaller and less fierce somehow, but their
eyes are still glowing in the dark like tiny
points of fire. As she sees you, Ferota lets out
a shriek and points her arm in your direction.
A burst of flame like a thunderbolt shoots out
from it and strikes the tree next to you. You
all jump into the woods just as more bolts
strike the trees around you.

"Yipes!" Thea cries, "this is as bad as the
maze of death we just went through."

In fact they are the thunderbolts of
death. You all dash through the woods
dodging them as they strike around you.

*Find your way through the thunderbolts
of death. One wrong move may be your last.*

Go to page 94

Go to page 124

Start

You've survived the attack of the thunderbolts. You dash out of the woods again and across another moonlit field. Ferota and Groar come out behind you. You brace yourself for a renewed attack. Ferota does extend her arm again—but this time nothing happens. She lets out a cry. It's no longer the cry of a sorceress, but that of a girl. You all stop in your tracks and look back. Both Ferota and Groar have shrunk down to half their sizes, and their fangs are gone.

"I think the same thing is happening to Ferota and Groar that happened to the demon in the jewel," you say. "They used up all their energy in that last attempt to stop us."

You, Thea, and Teppin walk back across the field toward the now shrunken figures. Groar ties to growl, but he sounds no fiercer than a small puppy. Ferota and Groar both sit down on the ground and start to cry.

"What do we do with these two now?" Teppin asks.

"I guess we'd better send Ferota back to her village and Groar to his father in the trees," you say.

"I don't fancy going all the way back to that side of the island," Teppin says. "I'd rather take my chances with pirates."

"Pirates!" Thea exclaims.

"So we've heard," you say.

"If there's anyone who knows how to handle pirates, it's me," Teppin says. "If we can get one of them to sail us away from this island. With the jewel as payment...."

"You'd give that dangerous thing to the pirates?" Thea says.

"I'm sure that by the time we get to their port," Teppin says, "there won't be any power left in it. In any event, the demon in the jewel is used to feeding on souls. He'll find precious few among the pirates."

Ferota and Groar are now the size of normal, young pygmies again. They are huddling together looking scared and confused.

"I don't think they even remember what they've been through," Teppin says.

"The poor things," Thea says, "I hope they can find their way."

"They'll be all right, I'm sure," you say.

You go over and try to tell them in sign language that all is forgiven and that they should return to their homes. You aren't sure if they understand or not, but they suddenly bolt across the field and disappear into the woods.

You, Thea, and Teppin rest there for awhile and watch the sun rise again. Then you get up and stretch, and head in the direction of where you think the pirate harbor should lie.

Ahead of you is a vast, swampy plain, criss-crossed with rivulets. You, Thea, and Teppin plod along the edges of these small waterways, sometimes slipping off and sinking up to your waists in the water. The going is rough and you make slow progress.

Suddenly, far ahead in one of the channels, you see a longboat with several figures in it. As you get closer you see that they are pirates. All of them, that is, except for one figure that appears to be tied up. When the pirates spot you, they start shouting and waving their hands indicating that you should come closer.

"Best we be on our guard," Teppin says.

"You mean you don't trust your friends over there," Thea says, laughing.

"Friends no more," Teppin says. "Though I do hope to find one with which we can make a deal."

Suddenly, you realize that you and Teppin are still wearing the robes of the Dirnls over the tattered remnants of your own clothes.

"Do you think we should take these off?" you ask Teppin.

"No," Teppin replies, "keep them on. I

have a hunch that it's a delegation of Dirnl
that they're expecting."

As you come up to the small boatload of
Pirates, they obviously look confused. They
can tell right away that you're not the usual
Dirnl types.

"Be ye from the sorceress?" one of them
calls out. "We bring a captive for her."

At this the captive, a young girl about
Thea's age, begins to sob hysterically. Thea
jumps into the water and wades over to the
boat.

"Don't worry," Thea tells her, "everything
is going to be all right."

"Not so fast!" shouts one of the pirates,
his cutlass slashing down at the gunwale of
the boat where Thea has her hand. "You don't
get the girl until we've got our gold."

Thea pulls her hand away just in time to
miss losing a few fingers. Her hand goes
straight to her whip and in the next instant,
she lashes out, the end of her whip curling
around the surprised priate's throat. Thea
jerks back on the whip and he goes flying
head first off the boat and into the water. His
cutlass plops into the water next to Teppin.
Teppin scoops it up and, with a quick motion,
pulls himself up into the boat. The two other
pirates charge at him. You get off a shot with
your slingshot that hits one of them in the

side of the head and he falls unconscious into the bottom of the boat. A few expert slashes and saber strokes from Teppin make the last pirate realize that he is outclassed. He leaps overboard where he is joined by the first one that Thea had toppled and they dash away, slipping and spalshing across the channels. Thea is already in the boat, untying the girl. It takes several minutes before the girl has quieted down enough to talk.

"My name is Tana," she says. "The ship I was travelling on was captured by pirates. I was brought here to be sold as a slave, or something like that."

"You're safe now," Thea says, not wanting to tell her just yet what the "something" was.

"We'll be safe as soon as we find our way through these channels and get back to the ocean," Teppin says, picking up a set of oars and handing one to you.

Go to next page.

Find your way through the maze of channels. Be careful, those pirates that ran off may be back when you're not looking.

Go to page 102

Go to page 107

Start

You made it through the channels. The last one empties into a wide, sheltered bay of the ocean. Far across on the other side you can see a small waterfront of sheds and low buildings. Several pirate ships are anchored close to it. The channel to the ocean is straight ahead.

"We're far enough away," Teppin says, "that the pirates on those ships may not notice us. They're probably all carousing in town anyway. But we'd better get out into the ocean fast. If we only had another pair of strong arms to help us...."

Then you hear a groaning in the bottom of the boat. The pirate that you knocked out is coming to.

"I think we just found them," you say, dashing water from a bucket over the pirate's head. He sits up, sputtering.

"Here, grab an oar," Teppin orders him, "we're going to make a run for it through that channel over there and you're going to help us."

The pirate, whose name you find out is Spike, turns out to be a very good rower. So with Teppin and Spike at one pair of oars, and you and Thea at another, you speed along through the water. Tana, is at the tiller following Teppin's shouted instructions.

Soon you are out into the ocean and

rounding the island. The pirates back in the bay don't seem to have seen you. After a full day of hard rowing, you are back near the high rocks and the pygmy village. You've been through the rocks before and this time you get through them easily and land on the beach. Your own ship is still there.

The pygmies, friendly this time, all come out to greet you. Tsing has returned to the village after seeing Groar reunited with his father. Ferota has returned to being a shepherdess. They are all grateful to you for freeing them from the tyranny of the jewel.

They all pitch in to help you repair your boat and stock it with provisions. Even Spike, now a friend, stays to help you before heading back across the island to find his ship.

A few days later, you find yourselves again out to sea, this time in your own boat. You now have an extra passenger, Tana, who you've promised to return to her own country. You've told her about the jewel.

"Can I see it?" Tana asks. "You've all told me so much about it."

You, Thea, and Teppin have been taking turns carrying it in its pouch, switching the carrier at the end of each day. But you haven't actually looked at the jewel itself for several days.

"Sure," Thea, whose turn it is, says.

She opens the pouch and holds it upside down to shake out the jewel. But only a stream of gray dust pours out and blows away in the wind. The jewel has disintegrated. You all look at each other in surprise, then burst into laughter. Somehow, it's a fitting end to an exciting adventure.

THE END

You do your best to keep the bow of the ship pointed into the waves. At times they seem to be coming from every direction. Suddenly, you look up and see another super-giant wave towering over you. This one is even bigger than the first. A chill of fear goes through you as you realize that your ship is broadside to it. You struggle desperately with the tiller to bring the bow into the wave. But it's too late. The wave crashes down on you, smashing your ship to pieces.

## THE END

*If you don't like this ending, go back to page 12 and try again.*

You and Teppin try to row with a steady rhythm. Thea and Tana sit in the bow, gazing intently ahead. Every so often, the boat comes to a halt as the water becomes too shallow. Sometimes you all jump overboard and push the boat into a deeper part of the channel. Other times you have to backtrack completely, looking for a way through. After a while, your attention is on the depth of the water and you forget to keep a lookout for pirates. Unfortuantely, the ones who ran away have been joined by others. They have been creeping up on you for some time. Now they suddenly attack.

Even though you and Teppin have been caught by surprise, you manage to beat off the first few that leap aboard the boat. But there are too many of them. While you are fighting off one bunch, others sneak up behind you. While one of the pirates climbs into the boat in front of you, another runs you through with his sword from behind.

## THE END

*If you don't like this ending, go back to page 100 and try again.*

The waves pound your ship from all directions. You ride up the side of each wave, reach the top, then plummet down again. At the bottom of a wave, you are in a deep trough while the water forms high walls around you. Each time a wave hits, it feels like your ship is going to be engulfed by the sea and never come up. Steadying the tiller is like holding on to a wild, thrashing beast. It takes all your strength to do it.

As you slide down the unusually steep side of a large wave, you realize, to your horror, that the ship isn't going to make it. It plunges into the sea and keeps going. An instant later you find yourself swimming alone in the sea. There's no sign of the ship.

Hour after hour, you are tossed around like a cork in the raging sea. It's a long way to land, and the storm is not nearly over. You are a strong swimmer but you can't last much longer.

## THE END

*If you don't like this ending, go back to page 12 and try again.*

Not only are huge waves smashing against the rocks all around you, but strong currents of water are rushing in between them, too. You row for all you're worth. It's tough going. The ship you're pulling, though small, is much larger than the tiny coracle. It's like a small child trying to lead a two hundred pound dog—a dog that doesn't want to go where the child wants it to go. You keep just barely missing the rocks, veering away at the last moment. Then a wave catches your ship and flings it through the air. Unfortunately, the small boat, with you in it, is also destroyed as the larger ship smashes into one of the rocks. Seconds later, nothing is left of either boat except small pieces tossed about by the surf.

### THE END

*If you don't like this ending, go back to page 20 and try again.*

You and Teppin struggle to find your way through the bushes. Soon, both of you are full of cuts and scratches. Your clothes are in tatters. You are in a desperate situation. No matter where you turn, the bushes and their terrible thorns leave less and less space for you to squeeze through between them. Trying to go back is just as difficult. The bushes seem to close in around you. Now you can't even find a passageway that you can get through. The thorns are digging deeper and deeper into your flesh. It's like being caught by a million sharp fish-hooks.

You struggle, but the more you do, the tighter you are caught. A black shadow crosses in the sky. You look up and see several buzzards circling around. You realize with horror what they are waiting for. You are to be their next meal—and they won't have long to wait.

### THE END

*If you don't like this ending, go back to page 28 and try again.*

You and Teppin crawl forward through the tunnel following Tsing. He can move faster than you can since he can stand upright. You see him way up ahead, the pale, greenish light from his insect cage glowing in the tunnel. Suddenly, Tsing screams and his light disappears completely.

"Tsing!" you call out. "Where are you?"

Your voice echos down thorugh the tunnel for a few seconds. Then all is silent.

Suddenly, you hear a pattering sound, like many small feet rushing toward you in the dark tunnel from both directions. Two mobs of pygmies are charging at you. Their rangs are usually not effective as weapons at close range, but in the narrow tunnel, you and Teppin don't have a chance. With dozens of pygmies slashing away at you, you don't last long.

### THE END

*If you don't like this ending, go back to page 38 and try again.*

You, Teppin, and Tsing work your way through the tunnels. Suddenly, you hear a strange sound up ahead. It's an angry, sucking sound. There's something about it that makes all of you freeze. A huge, ugly face appears in front of you. The head is as wide as you are tall and is mostly mouth and teeth. You realize with horror that it's the business end of one of the worm-like creatures. The rest of it must stretch back into the tunnel.

"I thought you said that all the sorm were out to sea at this season," you say to Tsing.

"I thought so," Tsing says, his voice shaking. "They must have left this one here to guard the tunnels."

Suddenly the creature moves forward and makes a grab for you with its gaping mouth. You roll back out of the way before it can close its jaws. Teppin jams his long knife into the creature's mouth. This only infuriates the creature and it rushes forward, its jaws snapping open and closed.

You all turn and try to get away, but you can't move fast enough in the narrow tunnel. The Sorm sucks you into its mouth, shredding you to pieces with its sharp teeth as it does.

### THE END

*If you don't like this ending, go back to page 38 and try again.*

You and Teppin search through the maze of passageways underneath the temple.

"I've a strange feeling that we've made a mistake coming down here," you say. "We're surrounded by evil forces, I can feel it."

"I can feel it too," Teppin says. "We'll retrace our steps and get back to the surface."

You turn around to go the other way when suddenly a section of wall drops from above, blocking off the corridor in front of you. Then another section closes behind you. You're trapped in between!

You and Teppin search along the walls on either side and also along the sections that just fell. All of them are smooth and unbroken except for a row of egg-sized holes just below the ceiling. You are standing there wondering what they are, when you find out! Streams of water start pouring out. Before you know it, you are standing up to your ankles in water, and the streams show no signs of stopping.

"The water must be coming from the lake above," Teppin says. "We're trapped."

Unfortunately, Teppin is right. The water rises to the top of the corridor. You hold your breath for as long as you can—which isn't long!

## THE END

*If you don't like this ending, go back to page 50 and try again.*

The basement of the monastery is a network of circular rooms connected by long passageways. These are as often as not blocked off, making a complicted series of dead ends. You and Teppin have to constantly retrace your steps.

Then, as you are crossing one of the rooms, you hear a growl that can only belong to Groar. It is coming toward you from one of the side passageways. You and Teppin hurry into the passageway opposite. You come to a blank wall! You try to run back the other way, but Groar is silhouetted in the doorway to the room. You are trapped!

You try to stop Groar with shots from your slingshot, but they just bounce off his head. Teppin tries to defend himself with his knife. The blade just glances off of Groar as if he were made of iron.

You make a last desperate attempt to run past Groar, but he grabs you by the neck with one hand and Teppin with the other. Then he smashes your two heads together.

### THE END

*If you don't like this ending, go back to page 80 and try again.*

You, Teppin and Tsing walk cautiously down the long tunnels of the mine. You go first, holding the torch ahead of you into the darkness. The floor is strewn with old timbers and, in places, the floor is planked over, covering the tops of vertical shafts.

"We'd better be careful," you say. "One of these shafts could be uncovered and we could stumble into it."

The tunnels themselves are confusing enough, and you are constantly coming to dead ends. Unfortunately, you start concentrating on solving the maze of passageways and forget about the floor.

You turn a corner and see a solid wall facing you. You are turning to go back and try a different tunnel, when you feel the floor giving way under you. You drop the torch and make a frantic dive for the solid part of the floor a couple of feet in front of you. But you are dropping too fast. You manage to grab a crossbeam at the edge of the shaft. But this pulls loose too, and you find yourself dropping helplessly into the dark abyss of the mine shaft. You fall for what seems like forever. But don't worry, you'll hit bottom soon.

## THE END

*If you don't like this ending, go back to page 58 and try again.*

You and Teppin move cautiously but quickly through the confusing maze of circular rooms and passageways under the monastery. You come to one dead end after another. All of these are blank walls closing off the passageways. All except one, that is. You come to a gate of heavy iron bars blocking your way. It appears to close by sliding out of the side of the wall. You and Teppin grab the bars and try to push it back in, but it doesn't budge.

Suddenly, a short way back down the corridor behind you, another gate slides out of the wall and blocks the passageway. You're trapped between them!

Then you see hundreds of tiny eyes glinting in the dim light beyond the bars on both sides of you. The small creatures start to squeal in anticipation. You realize with a shudder that they are rats. Scores of them. The bars to your cage are too close together for you to squeeze out, but they are just right for the rats to come pouring in. And the rats are hungry—very hungry!

### THE END

*If you don't like this ending, go back to page 80 and try again.*

The first tunnel is lit by narrow shafts of light beaming down from the entrance holes. Then tunnels branch off and go slightly downward into total darkness. Fortunately, there are stacks of unlit torches piled against one of the walls. Teppin quickly lights one with his flints, then using this to light two more, hands one to you and one to Tsing. You head deeper into the mines. You try to go in the direction of the forest. It isn't easy. You often have to retrace your steps in order to find the right passageway. Then you start hearing a strange sound, like picks chipping away at the walls of the mine. It's faint at first, but gets louder as you keep going.

"Didn't you say that these mines were no longer being worked?" you ask Tsing.

"That's what I've always heard," Tsing answers, "but I could be wrong."

"Well, there's definitely something going on down here," Teppin says, "and I intend to find out what it is."

As you go around the next corner, you see a line of pygmies with picks, chipping away at the wall. They are all shackled together with long chains attached to rings on their ankles. Then in front of you and behind you appear rows of Dirnl, holding deadly crossbows, loaded and cocked, and all pointed at you. For a moment, you think of fighting, but then you realize that you wouldn't stand a chance. You are helpless to do anything as the Dirnl attach chains to your ankles and hand you a pick. One of the guards gestures to you to start digging. You've arrived just in time for the next work-shift, scheduled to last for the next thirty years. If you do well enough on this shift, they may let you stay on for the next.

## THE END

*If you don't like this ending, go back to page 58 and try again.*

You and Teppin start out across the network of shaky rope bridges that go along the top of the forest. Below you is the thick screen of leaves, looking almost like solid ground. But you know that if you fall off of the walkway, you'll plummet through it and then down to the actual floor of the forest another hundred feet below. Above you in the sky, the clouds are now turning dark and ominous. Is it your imagination or can you see the outline of Ferota's face starting to form in the clouds. A wind springs up making the tops of the trees sway back and forth. You can almost hear Ferota's cruel laugh as the wind starts to whistle through the branches around you. The wind gets stronger and stronger. The bridges start to snap up and down. You hold on desperately as each violent move of the bridge threatens to throw you off.

Then, there is a loud snapping sound as the bridge you are on breaks away from the tree in front of you. You are swung in an arc down through the branches, still clinging to the ropes. You find yourself hanging down below the upper branches and high above the ground. Just as you start to climb up the rope, the other end of it breaks loose and you plummet with it down toward the ground.

## THE END

*If you don't like this ending, go back to page 70 and try again.*

You and Teppin search through the corridors under the temple. At first, there is an unearthly silence. Then you start to hear strange rustlings around the corners, the rustlings stop. Nothing is there. You go on, but you have a growing feeling of dread. It makes the hair stand up on the back of your neck. Then you find out that your fears are justified.

As you come to a four-way junction of the tunnels, giant, spider-like creatures suddenly appear from every direction. They come at you so fast that you and Teppin have almost no chance to defend yourselves. Teppin manages a few slashes with his long knife, but soon the creatures are dragging your lifeless bodies back to their lair.

## THE END

*If you don't like this ending, go back to page 50 and try again.*

You dash into the woods, trying to get away from the deadly thunderbolts. They're striking all around you. One hits the base of a tree right in front of you. You dive out of the way as it crashes to the ground, missing you by inches. As you are trying to get to your feet, another bolt topples the tree behind you. You roll sideways just as it falls in your direction. It misses you, but your foot is pinned under a heavy branch. Thea and Teppin dash toward you to help. But they are too late. The next tunderbolt is right on its target—you.

## THE END

*If you don't like this ending, go back to page 92 and try again.*

You and Teppin go in and out of the rock formations searching for a way through. No matter which way you turn, a stone structure blocks your way. Then, up ahead through a low arch, you see a broad, circular field. It has high, almost vertical, rock walls all around it.

"I wonder if there's a way through at the other side," you say.

"I don't know," Teppin says, "but there's something about it that I don't like. It's too perfect... almost like an arena."

You and Teppin go in anyway. You duck under the low arch and start cautiously across the open space. You haven't gotten more than a few yards when there is a grinding sound behind you. A large rock slides in front of the arch you just came through. At the same time, rows of hooded figures—Dirnl—suddenly appear at the top of the rock walls.

Then, at the other side of the field, a rock slides away from a large opening. Several huge, ugly beasts lumber out. They are easily twice your height and have enormous, gaping mouths bristling with long, sharp teeth.

A cry of anticipation goes up from the rows of spectators above as the beasts charge at you.

### THE END

*If you don't like this ending, go back to page 76 and try again.*

You and Teppin thread your way through the maze of rocks. Hundreds of strange sandstone shapes cover the floor of the valley—shapes carved by the flow of water sometime in the past. Many of them are beautiful, with veins of different colors running through the stone. But they are also maddening, making you double back again and again. Suddenly, you hear a growling and scraping on the stone not far away.

"Sounds like Groar isn't as hurt as we thought he was," Teppin says. "We'd better hide in another one of those rock caves until he goes past."

You find one nearby. This cave is even deeper than the one you had found before. You and Teppin crawl in, just as Groar, following your scent, comes around the corner of a rock in front of it. Groar stops at the entrance of the cave and sniffs.

"If he tries to come in after us, I'll get him with this," Teppin whispers, holding his long knife.

But Teppin doesn't get the chance. You listen in horror as Groar starts to slide some of the huge stones outside against the entrance to your cave—sealing you in.

## THE END

*If you don't like this ending, go back to page 76 and try again.*

You all rush through the fog, the flames exploding around you. In places the fog is a fine mist and you can run through it easily. Other places it seems to be just as thin, but it turns out to be as solid as rock. You keep having to make split second decisions as the flames burst all around you. Then, you think you see a way through. You dash between two columns of fog, but they turn out to be the solid kind. Suddenly you find yourself boxed in.

You try to run back, but the flames are already rushing toward you down the only escape route. You are forced back into the dead end, where the flames finally engulf you.

### THE END

*If you don't like this ending, go back to page 88 and try again.*

In the YOUR **AMAZING** adventures™ series, each book contains a new quest, new obstacles to be overcome, new mazes, and new dangers. And don't forget, *you* are the hero or heroine.

Now in print: